PEPPER
THE DRAGONFLY

Nancy P Best

WRITTEN BY NANCY PULLING BEST
ILLUSTRATED BY MATHEW S. CAPRON

Pepper The Dragonfly

by Nancy Pulling Best
Copyright © 2016

First Paperback Printing, February 2016
Second Paperback Printing, February 2023

Illustrations and Illustration Editing by Mathew S. Capron
Raleigh, North Carolina

Published by
PETRIE PRESS
A Division of Nancy Did It
2985 Powell Road
Blossvale NY 13308
nandidit@twcny.rr.com

Printed in the United States of America
by Versa Press

ISBN 978-0-9711638-6-7

Dedications

This book is dedicated to my older brother, Philip Earl Pulling. Pepper, as we called him, and I spent time together in the hospital back in 1954. We fought tuberculosis together and we both won the battle. But we lost him when he was only 26 years old.

   This one's for you Pep... because you were always pretty cool!

Nancy Pulling Best

This book is dedicated to my sister, Shawn Eileen Capron, who first inspired me to enjoy art with her own artistic creativeness. I miss her often. And to my daughter, who continues to inspire me to enjoy life everyday.

Mathew S. Capron

Pepper was a dragonfly. He was pretty cool.

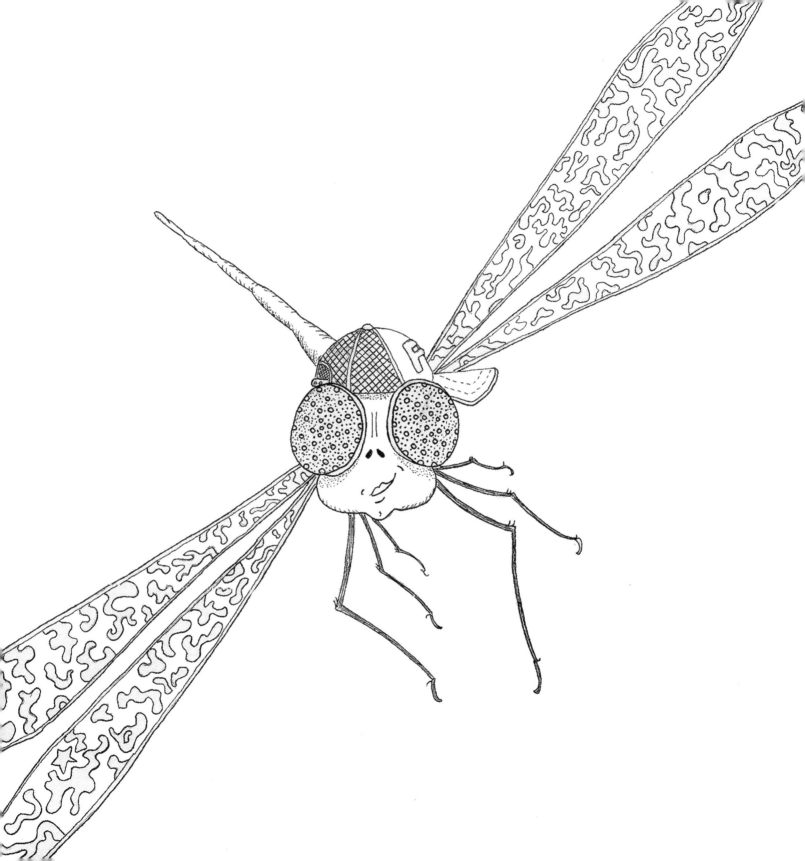

Pepper liked to fly across the top of Grandma's pool.

Sometimes he flew forward. Sometimes from side to side.

Every now and then
he'd give a
ladybug a ride.

Mosquitos were his favorite. He ate them by the dozens.

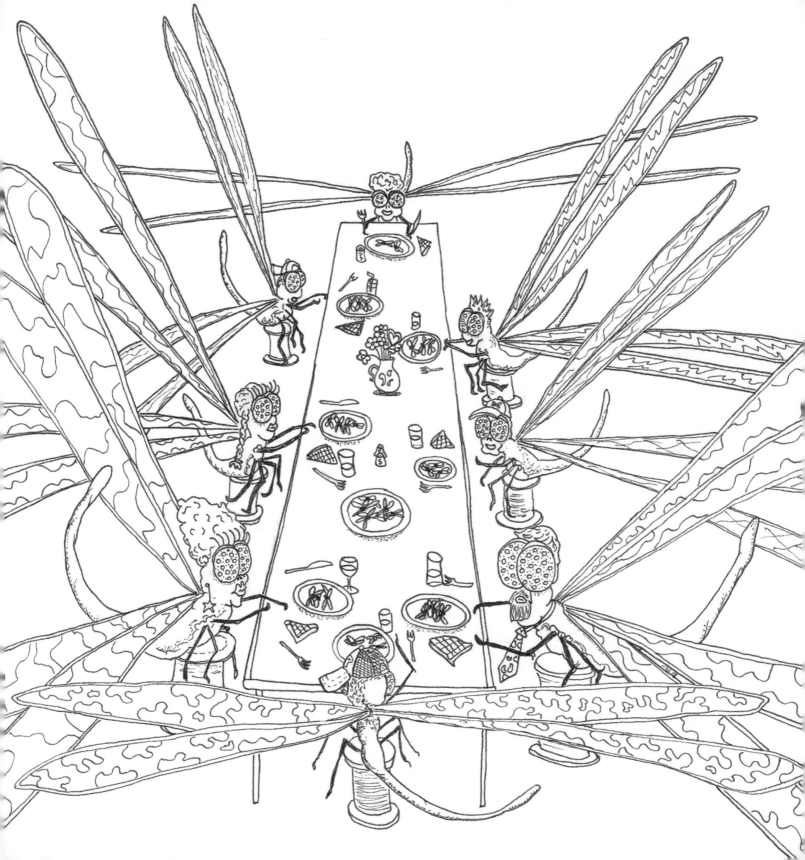

He ate them with his mom and dad and also with his cousins.

One day when Paul the pool guy was skimming out debris...

He bumped right into
Pep and broke a leg
or two or three.

Pep should have seen it coming with his enormous eyes.

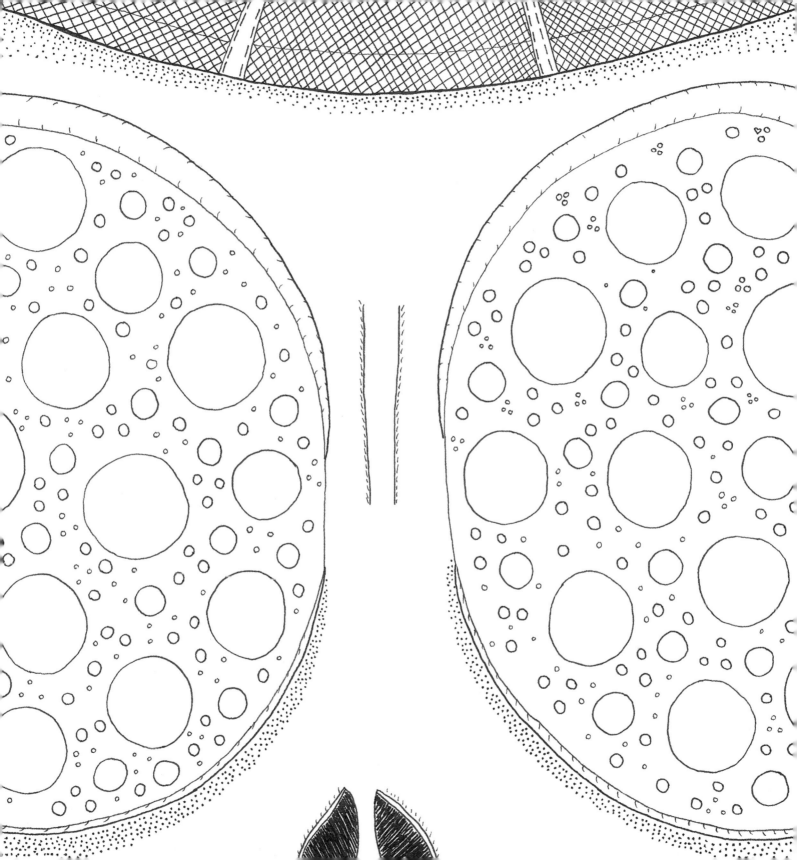

Because he could see in front, behind and even side to side.

The dragonfly was helpless, he couldn't do a thing.

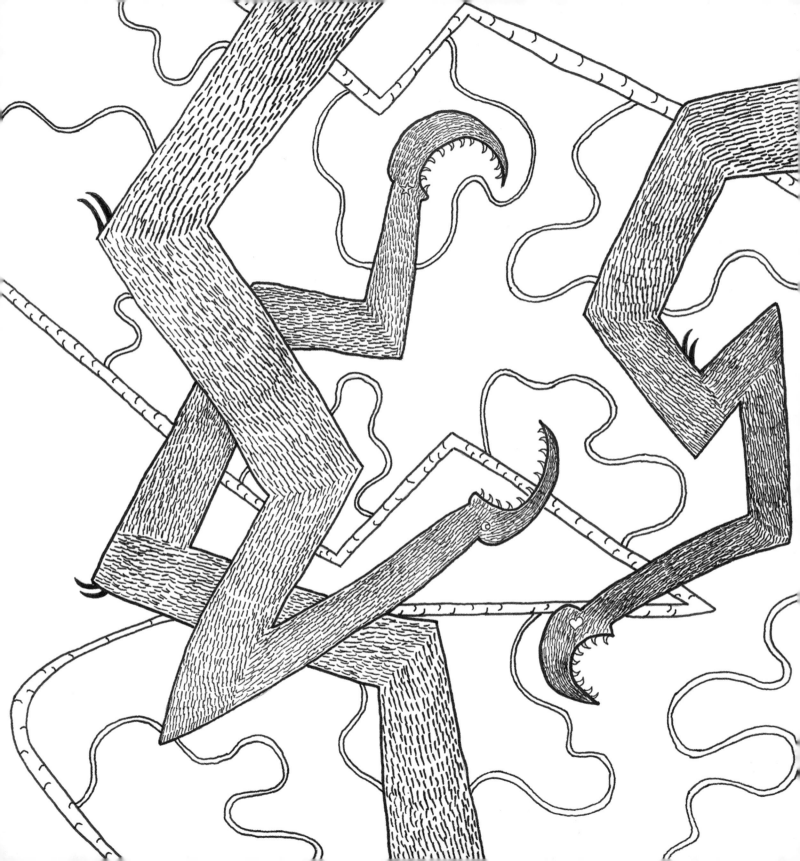

Pep had three broken legs and a badly battered wing.

The pool guy's youngest daughter took pity on the bug.

She wrapped up all his booboos and laid him on the rug.

She gathered up mosquitoes. Pep ate them with delight.

Within a few short weeks he was ready to take flight.

They drove him back
to Grandma's and
set him by the pool.

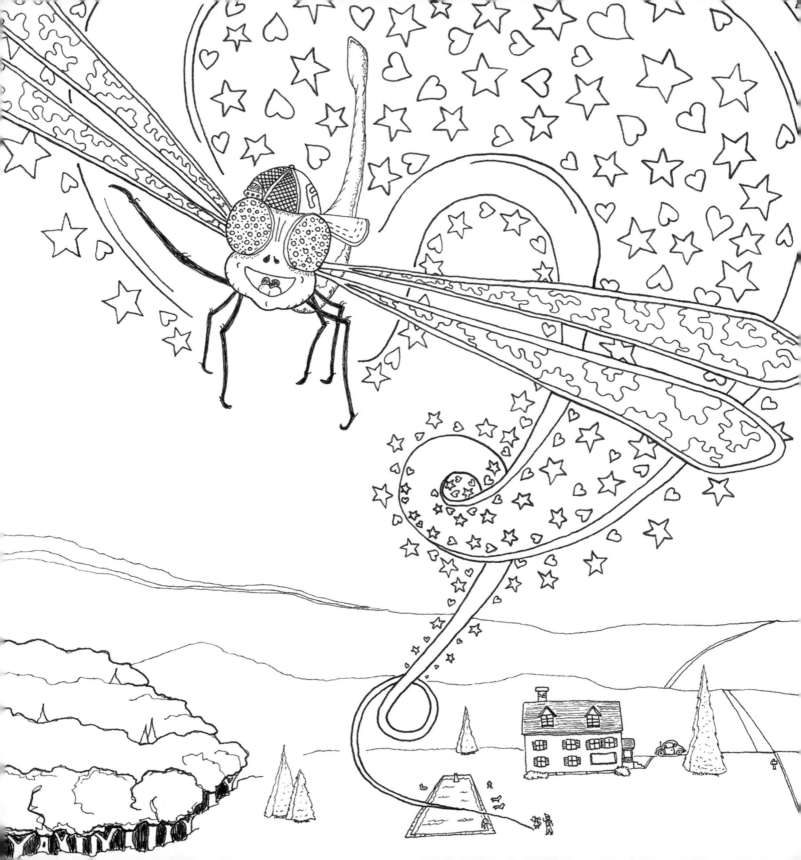

And when he took off that day, man, did he look cool!

MEET THE AUTHOR: Nancy Pulling Best

Born and raised in the Adirondack mountains in upstate New York, Nancy prides herself in being a 4th generation Adirondacker.

"My great grandparents, grandparents, parents, children and first grandchild were all from Old Forge, in the Adirondacks," Best said.

After writing for her own personal use, newspapers and magazines, she brings you her second children's book. She also authored *Anna The Spider, Learning To Cook Adirondack* and *Learning To Cook Adirondack Over An Open Fire*. They are all available at www.nancydidit.com

MEET THE ILLUSTRATOR: Mathew S. Capron

Born and raised in the Adirondack mountains in upstate New York, Mathew always had a love for art and found a lot of peace in it. He is the father of a beautiful daughter, who also enjoys being creative.

"I'm happy to have had an opportunity to illustrate this book," Mat said. "I hope you find happiness and peace within."

Mat also illustrated *Anna The Spider*. More art and illustrations by M@ can be found at... hew-Art.com

Pepper did all his own stunts during the making of This book and was not injured...